Tom & Small

For my Mum and Dad
with much love

Also by Clara Vulliamy: *Small*

First published in Great Britain by Collins Picture Books in 2004

1 3 5 7 9 10 8 6 4 2

ISBN: 0-00-713788-5

Collins Picture Books is an imprint of the Children's Division, part of HarperCollins Publishers Ltd.

Text and illustrations copyright © Clara Vulliamy 2004

The author/illustrator asserts the moral right to be identified as the author/illustrator of the work.
A CIP catalogue record for this title is available from the British Library.

The HarperCollins website address is: www.harpercollins.co.uk

Printed and bound in China

Tom & Small

Clara Vulliamy

((Collins

An imprint of HarperCollins*Publishers*

Tom is going to big school tomorrow for the very first time.
That night, Tom and Mum try out all his new things.
"You're going to look so grown-up," Mum tells him.

He has a new sweatshirt...

new shoes with
spaceships on them...

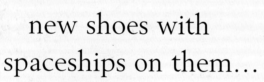

a shiny notebook,
some special pens...

and a new red bag…

to put his apple and
drink in, for break time,

and a special pocket
to keep Small.

"Tom," says Mum, helping him into his pyjamas, "Small is too precious to take to school. He might get lost. It's best to leave him at home."

Mum tucks Tom up in bed and gives him a kiss.

"Off to sleep now.
It's a big day tomorrow.
Sweet dreams."

But Tom can't sleep.

He holds Small closely and asks him,
"Will I be scared at school?
Will I miss you too much?
I don't think I want to be big and grown-up.
I want to stay at home, with you."
Small understands.

At last, Tom closes his eyes.
But he is restless, tossing and turning.

And then…

a little voice calls out his name.

Tom reaches down and feels himself falling...

falling…

falling…

falling…

until he cries out, "Small, look, I'm just like you!"

"Come on, Tom, come
with me and play!"

Speeding down
the tracks…

tunnelling through…

jumping from note to
note on Tom's little
piano…

roaring at the
dinosaurs…

hurtling around
on a skateboard.

Inside the dolls' house, a tea party for Tom and
new clothes for Small...

up the ladder to bounce on the beds...

Then, "This way, quick,
let's see if we can fly!"

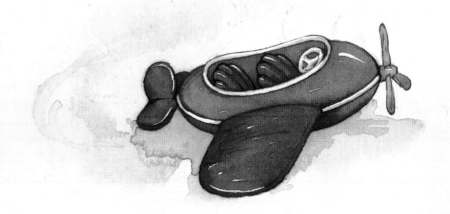

Into the plane, up and round and round and round the room, then...

"Shall we?"
"YES!"
Out of the window…

soaring up over the houses, the treetops, past a big silver moon...

"Look! There – down there," calls out Tom,
"that's my school!"

They dip down through the branches
and fly past the window,

looking in at all the books
and games and paints and toys.

"I can see my peg with my name on it, all ready for me...

and where I'll sit, and a special place for all my things."

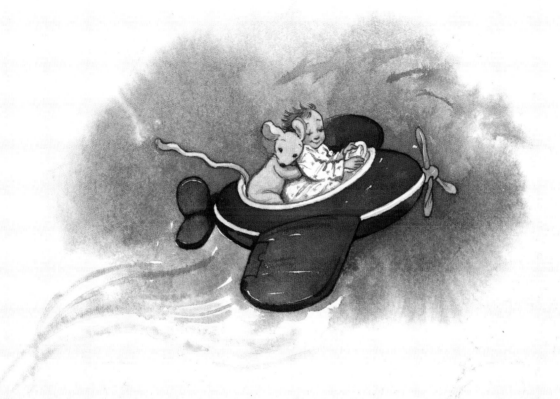

"Just waiting for when you arrive
in the morning," says Small.
"And now I think it's time to go home."

"Can we do this again, every night?"
Tom asks sleepily, as they get back into bed.
"Yes, every night."
"Always?"
"Always."

Everything is going to be all right, thinks
Tom, and he yawns the biggest yawn
and falls asleep with Small
in his arms.

Tom is very quiet walking to school
with Mum the next morning.

At the gate, he takes Small
out of Mum's bag to say goodbye.
Mum tells him, "We'll be here,
me and Small, to pick you up
at going home time."

In the playground,
something catches Tom's eye.

It's the tiny scarf that Small
borrowed from the dolls' house.
He must have dropped it in the night.
"I *knew* it wasn't a dream," says Tom.

Tom is so busy,
playing games,

chatting and looking
at books,

exploring the playground

and painting his picture
to go on the wall.

In no time at all, Mum
and Small are back.

"How was your first day, Tom?"
"It wasn't a bit scary, and Mum...

…can I come back tomorrow?"